First published in 2001 in Great Britain by

Gullane Children's Books

This book & CD edition published in 2007 by

Gullane Children's Books

Winchester House, 259-269

Old Marylebone Road, London NW1 5XJ

1 3 5 7 9 10 8 6 4 2

Illustrations © Jane Cabrera 2001

The right of Jane Cabrera to be identified

as the illustrator of this work has been

asserted by her in accordance

with the Copyright, Designs,

For Paula

and Patents Act, 1988.

A CIP record for this title is available

from the British Library.

ISBN !3: 978-1-86233-686-5

ISBN 10: 1-86233-686-5

Printed and bound in China

Jane Cabrera

Old Mother Hubbard

GULLANE
CHILDREN'S BOOKS

Old Mother Hubbard went to the cupboard

But when she got there, the cupboard was bare, and so the poor dog had none

She went to
the tailor's

to buy him
a coat

But when she came back, he was riding a goat

She went to
the hatter's

to buy him
a hat

But when she
came back,
he was washing
the cat

She went to
the barber's

to buy him
a wig

She went to
the cobbler's

to buy him
some shoes

But when
she came back,
he was reading
the news

Other Gullane Children's Books
illustrated by Jane Cabrera

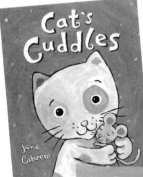

Cat's Cuddles

Mummy Carry Me Please!

Ten in the Bed

Over in the Meadow

If You're Happy and You Know It!

Eggday
JOYCE DUNBAR (AUTHOR)

Other titles available with sing-along CD

If You're Happy and You Know It!